# Hiccup!

Published in 2012
by Wayland

Text copyright © Jillian Powell 2010
Illustration copyright © Mark Chambers 2010

Wayland
338 Euston Road
London NW1 3BH

Wayland Australia
Level 17/207 Kent Street
Sydney, NSW 2000

Series Editor: Louise John
Editor: Katie Powell
Cover design: Paul Cherrill
Design: D.R.ink
Consultant: Shirley Bickler

A CIP catalogue record for this book is available from the British Library.

ISBN 9780750261968

First published in 2010, reprinted in 2012.

Printed in China

Wayland is a division of Hachette Children's Books,
an Hachette UK Company
www.hachette.co.uk

# Hiccup!

Written by Jillian Powell
Illustrated by Mark Chambers

WAYLAND

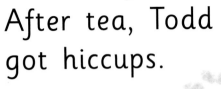

After tea, Todd
got hiccups.

"Hiccup! Hiccup!"

"Try holding your nose and counting to ten," said Mum.

That didn't work.

"Hiccup! Hiccup!"
said Todd.

"Try holding your arms up in the air," said Dad.

But it didn't work.

"Hiccup! Hiccup!"
said Todd.

"Stand on your hands!"
said Tilly.

"That won't work,"
said Todd.

"Now drink this water!"
said Mum.

"Hiccup! Hiccup!"
said Todd.

"Sugar will do it!"
said Dad.

"Sugar?" said Mum.
"That won't work!"

"Hiccup! Hiccup!"
said Todd.

"I know what to do!"
said Tilly.

She went to get a sheet
from the cupboard.

"Boo!" shouted Tilly.

"That didn't scare me,"
said Todd. "Hiccup Hiccup!"

But Tilly did scare Barney.
He began to bark.

"Shush!" said Todd. He put his fingers in his ears.

Pop! The hiccups stopped.

"No more hiccups!" said Todd. "Good dog, Barney!"

START READING is a series of highly enjoyable books for beginner readers. **The books have been carefully graded to match the Book Bands widely used in schools.** This enables readers to be sure they choose books that match their own reading ability.

## Look out for the Band colour on the book in our Start Reading logo.

The Bands are:

Pink Band 1A & 1B

Red Band 2

Yellow Band 3

Blue Band 4

Green Band 5

Orange Band 6

Turquoise Band 7

Purple Band 8

Gold Band 9

START READING books can be read independently or shared with an adult. They promote the enjoyment of reading through satisfying stories supported by fun illustrations.

**Jillian Powell** began writing stories when she was four years old. She lives in a house beside a village church and sits down to write every day. She has written stories and rhymes about dogs, cats, scarecrows and crocodiles as well as children such as Tilly and Todd.

**Mark Chambers** lives in Lincoln. His studio, where he illustrates, is full of books, drawings and posters and is home to a lobster called Larry!